For Daddy & Kayley Jane
on your 1st Fathers Day.
June 2005

To Briony M.K.
For Emilia, with lots of love K.M.

OXFORD
UNIVERSITY PRESS

Great Clarendon Street, Oxford OX2 6DP

Oxford University Press is a department of the University of Oxford.
It furthers the University's objective of excellence in research, scholarship,
and education by publishing worldwide in

Oxford New York

Auckland Bangkok Buenos Aires Cape Town Chennai
Dar es Salaam Delhi Hong Kong Istanbul Karachi Kolkata
Kuala Lumpur Madrid Melbourne Mexico City Mumbai Nairobi
São Paulo Shanghai Taipei Tokyo Toronto

Oxford is a registered trade mark of Oxford University Press in
the UK and in certain other countries

British Library Cataloguing in Publication Data available

ISBN 0-19-279123-0 (hardback)
ISBN 0-19-272555-6 (paperback)

1 3 5 7 9 10 8 6 4 2

Printed in China

Where's My Darling Daughter?

By Mij Kelly

Illustrated by

Katharine McEwen

OXFORD
UNIVERSITY PRESS

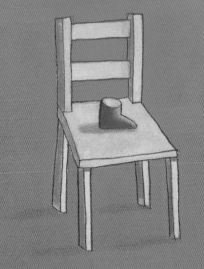

Poppa Bombola
looked in the cot –
looked in the cot and
got such a shock!

'Where's my darling
daughter?'

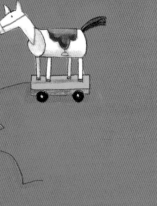

He looked on the table and under the chairs.

He looked everywhere.
High and low he sought her.
'I know I put her somewhere safe,
but I've lost my darling daughter!'

Poppa Bombola ran out the back –
ran out the back in a terrible flap.
'I've lost my daughter,' he told the cat.
He looked under the mat.

He looked under
the cat!

'I know I put her somewhere safe.
Oh, where's my darling daughter?'

Poppa Bombola ran to the pond –
right into the pond with
his best boots on.

'I've lost my daughter,' he told the duck,
as he waded and wallowed
and slipped in the muck.

'I know I put her somewhere safe.
Oh, where's my
darling daughter?'

Poppa Bombola ran to the shed –
ran to the shed with his heart full of dread.
'I've lost my daughter,' he told the cow.
'Don't ask me how – I haven't
got time to talk to you now.

I know I put her somewhere safe.
Oh, where's my darling daughter?'

Poppa Bombola ran to the sty –
ran to the sty with tears in his eyes.
'I've lost my daughter,' he told the pig.

'I'm running around, all in a tizz.
Do you know where my daughter is?
I'm sure I put her somewhere safe.

Oh, where's my darling daughter?'

Poppa Bombola sat down and cried – he covered his
eyes and he cried and he cried.

'Oh, where's my
darling daughter?'

He'd searched his farm high and low.
Everywhere he'd sought her.
He knew he'd put her somewhere safe,

but he'd lost his darling daughter.

Poppa Bombola rubbed his eyes –

rubbed his eyes and ...

...what a surprise!
'You found my darling daughter!'

'Oh, thank you, thank you,
and thank you again,'

he told the
cow and the cat,
the pig,
duck, and hen.